RAINBOW magic ®

The Petal Fairies

To Lily Grace Evans, who
will always believe in fairies

Special thanks to
Sue Mongredien

ORCHARD BOOKS
338 Euston Road, London NW1 3BH
Orchard Books Australia
Hachette Children's Books
Level 17/207 Kent Street, Sydney, NSW 2000

A Paperback Original

HiT entertainment

First published in 2007 by Orchard Books
Rainbow Magic is a registered trademark of Working Partners Limited.
Series created by Working Partners Limited, London W6 0QT

Text © Working Partners Limited 2007
Cover illustrations © Georgie Ripper 2007
Inside illustrations © Orchard Books 2007

A CIP catalogue record for this book is available from the British Library.

ISBN 978 1 84616 457 6

3 5 7 9 10 8 6 4 2

Printed and bound in China by Imago

Orchard Books is a division of Hachette Children's Books

www.orchardbooks.co.uk

Tia the Tulip Fairy

by Daisy Meadows

ORCHARD BOOKS

www.rainbowmagic.co.uk

The Fairyland Palace

Blossom Hall

Fairy Garden

Leafley Village

Visitors' Centre

I need the magic petals' powers,
To give my castle garden flowers.
And so I use my magic well
To work against the fairies' spell.

From my wand ice magic flies,
Frosty bolt through fairy skies.
And this crafty spell I weave
To bring the petals back to me.

Contents

A Fairy Garden

"I think the Fairy Garden must be through here," Rachel Walker said, pointing to a wrought-iron gate. She and her friend, Kirsty Tate, were exploring the grounds of Blossom Hall, an old Tudor house hotel, where their families were staying over the Easter holidays. Both girls had been interested

to hear the owner of Blossom Hall,
Mrs Forrest, speak about the history
of the house and garden as she'd served
their breakfast that morning. And
they had been particularly intrigued
when Mrs Forrest had mentioned the
Fairy Garden. After all, Kirsty and
Rachel knew a lot about fairies: they
were friends with them!

"It's known as the
Fairy Garden because
there is a perfect ring
of tulips growing in
the middle of it,"
Mrs Forrest had
explained. "We
call it the Blossom
Fairy Ring. And you've
come at just the right time of year.

The tulips are blooming and they look lovely, even though I don't think they're quite as bright and beautiful as they were last year."

As soon as they'd finished their breakfast, Rachel and Kirsty had asked their parents if it was all right for them to go exploring. They'd arrived at Blossom Hall the night before, and were eager to look around during the sunny morning. From the breakfast room, the gardens looked very pretty, with their pink and white flowering cherry trees, long rolling lawns, and masses of cheerful flowers.

"Of course you can explore," Mr Tate had said. "Just make sure you stay within the high wall that runs all the way around Blossom Hall and its gardens."

Mrs Forrest had told the girls to follow the winding path that led through a copse of trees at the back of the house. "You'll come to a walled garden, with a gate in one side," she'd said.

"The Fairy Garden is in there."

Rachel lifted the latch of the gate,
eagerly. "Here we are!" she said,
pushing it open.

The girls stepped into the walled
garden together. "Isn't it gorgeous?"
Kirsty exclaimed, her eyes taking in the
rambling roses that climbed the walls,
and the old stone fountain in one corner.

"It's just the sort of place you can imagine a real fairy visiting," Rachel said, smiling. "And that must be the Blossom Fairy Ring!" she added,

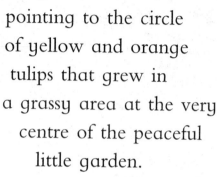

pointing to the circle of yellow and orange tulips that grew in a grassy area at the very centre of the peaceful little garden.

"How pretty!" Kirsty said, going over for a closer look, and noticing that some of the tulips were wilting. But then she stopped and listened intently. "Rachel, can you hear someone crying?" she asked in a whisper.

Rachel stood quite still, listening hard, then nodded as she too heard the faint sound of sobs. "I can't see anyone else here, though," she whispered back, gazing around. "Who could it be?"

The girls looked around the small garden, but it wasn't big enough to have many hiding places. Then, as Kirsty was walking past the tulips of the fairy ring, she paused. The crying was definitely louder there. It seemed to be coming from the tulips.

Kirsty looked inside the nearest tulip.

And then she gasped. Sitting at the bottom of the flower, with her face in her hands, was a tiny fairy!

Kirsty beckoned to Rachel, then crouched down by the flower. "Hello," she said gently. "I'm Kirsty. What's wrong?"

The fairy gave a gulp and looked up at Kirsty. She had long brown wavy hair and was wearing a cute white and orange outfit with a pretty tulip

necklace and little dark
orange shoes.

"Hello," she said,
sadly. "I'm Tia
the Tulip Fairy,
and I'm looking
for my magic petal."

"Hi, Tia," said
Rachel, crouching next
to Kirsty. "Maybe we can help you
find the petal?" she suggested. "We've
helped lots of other fairies before."

Tia looked from Rachel to Kirsty, and
her face brightened. "Rachel and Kirsty?
I've heard all about you," she said.
"Oh, thank goodness I've met you!"

Kirsty smiled. "What happened to
your petal?" she asked. "How did
it get lost?"

Tia got to her feet. "It's quite a long story. I might need some help explaining," she said. As she spoke, she sprinkled a handful of orange, petal-shaped fairy dust over the girls, and before they quite knew what was happening, they found themselves shrinking until they were the same size as Tia.

"We're fairies!" exclaimed Rachel, flapping the shimmering wings on her back in delight. Then she noticed that the Fairy Garden was blurring in front of her eyes.

She just had time to grab Kirsty's hand before she felt herself being pulled through the air, very fast. "Where are we going?" she cried, feeling a rush of excitement.

"To Fairyland, of course!" Tia called back.

Petal Thieves

After a few moments, the girls felt themselves slowing down, and then they landed on the ground. They were standing in front of the palace, its towers and turrets gleaming in the sunshine. Nearby stood the King and Queen of Fairyland, along with a group of other fairies that Kirsty and Rachel didn't recognise.

"Hello, Your Majesties," Kirsty said, curtseying politely. She and Rachel had been to Fairyland many times to help the fairies, but it still gave her a feeling of awe every time she saw King Oberon and Queen Titania.

The King and Queen both smiled. "We're so pleased to see you again," the King told the girls.

"You're just in time to help," the Queen added.

"What's happened?" Rachel asked.

The smile slipped from the King's face. "I'm afraid Jack Frost has been up to his tricks again," he said gravely. "This time, he's been causing trouble for our Petal Fairies."

Rachel and Kirsty exchanged glances. Spiky Jack Frost was always up to mischief in the fairy world.

"What has he done now?" Kirsty asked.

"Well, he was upset that none of the beautiful flowers of Fairyland would grow in the cold ground around his ice castle," the Queen explained. "So he sent his goblins to steal the Petal Fairies' magic petals, hoping that their powerful Petal Magic would help."

"Here are our Petal Fairies," the King said, introducing them one by one. "You've met Tia the Tulip Fairy, and this is Pippa the Poppy Fairy, Louise the Lily Fairy, Charlotte the Sunflower Fairy, Olivia the Orchid Fairy, Danielle the Daisy Fairy and Ella the Rose Fairy."

The Petal Fairies all gave small smiles of welcome, but Kirsty and Rachel couldn't help noticing how sad they looked.

"Let's go to the seeing pool," the Queen suggested. "We can show you how it all happened."

The girls followed the fairies through the palace gardens to the magical seeing pool. The Queen waved her wand over the water, and it shimmered all the colours of the rainbow as a picture formed on its surface.

Kirsty and Rachel stared at the images forming in the pool, and saw a group of Jack Frost's goblin servants sneaking into the palace gardens. The sun was just rising, and one of the goblins was yawning and stretching.

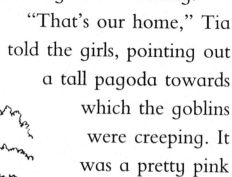

"That's our home," Tia told the girls, pointing out a tall pagoda towards which the goblins were creeping. It was a pretty pink colour, and had little golden balconies and a sparkling golden roof.

"We sleep on the top three floors, and the ground floor is our summerhouse."

"That's where the magic petals are kept," Charlotte put in.

"Were kept, you mean," Olivia said sadly. "Until this morning…"

The girls watched as the goblins tiptoed through the doors of the summerhouse. Moments later, they emerged with gleeful smiles on their faces and seven colourful petals, each the size of an apple, in their hands.

"Jack Frost is going to be so pleased with us when we get these back to the ice castle," the first goblin smirked, waving an orange petal above his head in triumph.

Tia let out a groan as she watched. "That's my magic petal. Look at the way he's whirling it around!" she said in anguish. "He's not taking proper care of it at all!"

Rachel squeezed her hand to try and comfort her as they watched what happened next.

The other goblins were all looking amazed as a stream of orange tulips floated out from the magic petal, and

planted themselves in the ground nearby! "Hey!" shouted one goblin with an especially long nose. "How did you do that?"

The goblin with the orange petal stopped and stared at the mass of tulips that had appeared. "I just…waved it," he said in surprise. "Like this." He shook the petal again, and another stream of tulips, pink ones this time, appeared, and planted themselves beneath a tree.

"Wow!" the long-nosed goblin marvelled. He held up the yellow petal that he was holding.

"That's mine," Charlotte the Sunflower Fairy told Kirsty and Rachel crossly.

The long-nosed goblin wiggled the yellow petal experimentally, and, seconds later, a crop of sunflowers had sprung up at his feet. He jumped back in surprise and then chuckled. "This is great!" he said, in excitement. "Where else can we grow flowers?"

Before long, all the goblins were playing about with the magic petals. Purple flowers sprang up round tree trunks, red

ones blossomed in a stream
the goblins passed, and a
big white daisy appeared
on one goblin's head!
"And while those
goblins were
meddling with
the Petal
Magic," the
Queen said
disapprovingly
from the side of
the seeing pool,
"our Petal Fairies
woke up and
realised that their
petals had been stolen."
"And we wanted them back!"
Ella the Rose Fairy declared.

"When the magic petals are in their places in the pagoda," put in Louise the Lily Fairy, "our wands are automatically topped up each morning with Petal Magic. Of course, that didn't happen this morning because the petals were stolen, but we still had a little Petal Magic left. So we used the last drops in a spell to draw the magic petals back to us."

In the pool, Kirsty and Rachel could see the effect of the fairies' spell.

The petals were swept out of the goblins' hands, and carried back towards the fairies in a sparkly, pink stream of magic, high in the air.

The goblins looked alarmed. "Quick, get them back!" one of them shouted, rushing after the petals.

The others followed, running along and jumping up, trying to grab the floating petals. "Jack Frost will be cross if he finds out we let them go!" one of the goblins panted.

"He certainly will!" boomed a voice just then, and the girls saw that Jack Frost had appeared behind the goblins, looking furious.

He muttered a few magic words, and waved his wand in the air, sending an icy bolt of magic shooting straight towards the petals.

Goblins Get Magic

Boom! Jack Frost's icy magic collided with the pink Petal Magic, and there was an enormous explosion of pink petals and dazzling white and silver snowflakes. The magic petals flew in all directions, like sparks from a firework. Then they disappeared from view.

"Where did they go?" Rachel asked.

The Petal Fairies exchanged glances.

"That's the problem," Tia replied.

"They're lost in the human world," the King explained. "But we don't know where!"

"We'll help you find them," Kirsty put in at once. She felt tingly at the thought of another fairy adventure.

The King and Queen smiled at the girls.

"We were hoping you'd say that," the Queen said warmly, "because without the petals, the Petal Fairies can't work their magic and make new flowers grow."

"It also means that all the flowers already in bloom will die more quickly," the King put in sadly.

"That's awful," Kirsty said. She could hardly imagine what the world would look like without flowers. The gardens of Blossom Hall would certainly seem bare and her own garden at home would no longer be full of colour!

"We'll do our best to help you get the magic petals back," Rachel promised the Petal Fairies.

The Queen waved her wand over the seeing pool again. "There's just one more thing I need to show you before you go…"

Kirsty and Rachel watched the pool as colours rippled across the surface, and the picture changed. Now they saw Jack Frost in the great hall of his ice castle, instructing his servants to find the magic petals.

"I order you to stay together," he told

the goblins firmly. "And do whatever you have to do to bring the petals back to me. That includes using this..." He handed a magic wand to the goblin nearest him. The goblin took the glittering silver wand, a grin spreading over his face. "Thank you," he said gleefully. "It's charged with my own powerful magic," Jack Frost explained. "And it's to make sure you don't get outwitted by those fairies again. Don't let me down!"

The goblins all nodded eagerly.

"You must take great care," the King warned Kirsty and Rachel as the picture faded. "The goblins will be in one big group and with a wand full of

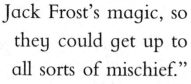

Jack Frost's magic, so they could get up to all sorts of mischief." Rachel nodded solemnly. "We'll be careful," she promised, biting her lip. Just then, Tia stepped forward. "I thought I could sense my tulip petal near Blossom Hall — that's why you found me there," she explained. "Perhaps we could go back to look there first?"

"Of course," Kirsty said at once.

Pippa the Poppy Fairy was nodding. "Once that petal has been found, tulips will be safe at least," she said. She turned to the girls. "Each petal governs its own particular flower, and flowers of a particular colour," she told them. "So Tia's orange petal makes the tulips grow, but also every other orange-coloured flower, like marigolds. When all seven magic petals are together in place in Fairyland, they make all the flowers in the world grow."

Kirsty and Rachel turned to Tia.
"What are we waiting for?"
Rachel asked.

"Let's go back to Blossom Hall
and start searching!" Kirsty added.

Tia smiled gratefully. Then she waved
her wand, sending a flurry of fairy dust
swirling all around the three of them.

Kirsty and Rachel only just had time to call out goodbye to the King, Queen and the Petal Fairies before they were swept up in a whirl of glittering colours.

They were off on another exciting fairy adventure!

It's Raining Petals

When the magic whirlwind died down, Rachel and Kirsty found themselves standing on one of the lawns of Blossom Hall, and they were girls again.

Tia fluttered in mid-air in front of them. "Let's get looking!" the little fairy called, her wings a shimmering blur as she flew towards the nearest flowerbed.

"I'm sure the magic Tulip Petal is somewhere nearby. I can just feel it."

The three of them began searching a row of flowerbeds – Tia from the air, Rachel and Kirsty walking carefully along the edge – all hoping to spot the bright orange petal. Kirsty couldn't help noticing that some of the flowers were looking rather wilted, and there were a few bare spaces where nothing was growing.

Tia noticed her staring at the bare patches of earth. "There should be some lilies and irises coming up there," she told the girls, "but they haven't started growing yet, because the Lily Petal is lost." She pointed to another clear patch. "Soon, there should be the most gorgeous poppies over there," she said, looking sad again, "but if Pippa doesn't get her Poppy Petal back, then..." her voice trailed off sadly.

Rachel stared at the bare ground, feeling sad. They had to find the magic petals, and the sooner the better!

Once they'd checked the flowerbeds, the girls and Tia headed over to a rockery. Unfortunately, there was no sign of the magic Tulip Petal there, either, nor was it anywhere to be seen by the tinkling fountains.

"There's an apple orchard," Kirsty said, pointing. "Should we try there?"

"Good idea," Rachel said, walking towards it. "Oh, aren't the trees gorgeous with all their blossom?"

The others agreed. Delicate sprays of the pinky-white flowers lined the branches of the apple trees.

"And that one is even prettier than the others," Kirsty said, pointing out a tree a few metres away that was absolutely covered in blossom. "I wonder why it's flowering so well?" A thought struck her and she stopped, staring excitedly at Tia. "You don't think

it's something to do with your petal's magic powers, do you?"

Tia's eyes lit up. "It might be, Kirsty. Let's have a closer look!" she said.

The girls and Tia hurried towards the tree, but came to a sudden halt when they spotted Jack Frost's band of goblins underneath it!

The goblins were all shaking the trunk of the tree as hard as they could, sending showers of apple blossom tumbling down like confetti.

"What are they doing that for?" Rachel wondered aloud.

"My petal! It's there, in the tree!"

Tia cried suddenly, pointing to
a high branch.

Rachel and Kirsty looked up and
noticed a bright orange petal stuck in
the topmost branches of the tree. It was
much larger than a real petal, Kirsty
noticed. It was almost as big as her
own hand.

"They're shaking the tree to try and
dislodge the petal," Rachel realised.
"We've got to get it before they do!"

Tia waved her wand over the girls, and they shrank to become fairies once more.

"Let's try and fly up to the petal without the goblins seeing us," Tia suggested. "But watch out for the falling blossom!"

"Okay," Kirsty said, fluttering her wings. "Let's go!"

She and Rachel followed their fairy friend as she dodged nimbly through the falling petals. *It's just like flying through a blizzard of perfumed snowflakes*, Rachel thought, as she zoomed upwards.

"Keep shaking!"
one of the goblins
shouted from
down below, still
rocking the tree trunk.
"It's got to fall soon!"

"Not if we can get it first," Kirsty
muttered, fluttering her wings faster
than ever. She, Rachel and Tia were
closing in on the petal now, but, just
then, Kirsty heard a loud shout.

"Hey! What's that up there?"

Kirsty glanced down to see all the
goblin faces glaring up at her. She'd
been spotted.

A Silly Spell

The three fairies arrived next to the petal, grabbed hold of it and tried to pull it away from the tree, but it was stuck fast on a twig.

Rachel could see that one of the goblins was pointing Jack Frost's wand up at them.

"I reckon we should try this out," he

suggested to his friends. "Anyone know any good spells?"

"Just make something up!" another goblin advised. "Say something that sounds magical."

"Let's try shaking the petal loose," urged Tia quickly. "I don't like the sound of this!"

The three fairies jiggled and shook the soft, smooth petal until it suddenly came away from the twig.

"Let's go!" Rachel cried.

But before they could fly away with the petal, the goblin with the wand started chanting.

"Pesky fairies, that's enough!

I conjure up a…" he paused and looked doubtful. "What shall I conjure up?" he asked his friends.

"A wind that's rough!" shouted a different goblin with mean eyes. "Let's blow them away!"

"No chance," Tia spluttered. "I've never heard such rubbish spell-casting!"

"It might be rubbish, Tia," Rachel said anxiously, peering down. "But it seems to be working!"

The three fairies all cried out in alarm
as a great stream of icy wind flooded
from Jack Frost's wand straight
towards them. As it reached them,
it swept them high into the air.

"Hold tight to the petal!"
Kirsty shouted, but the
wind whipped the words
from her mouth, and
then ripped the petal
right out of her hands.

Rachel and Tia, too,
found it impossible to cling on to the
edges of the petal,
and the three
fairies were
flung into the
branches of
another tree.

They watched
helplessly as the
wind carried the
petal up and
away from them,
higher and higher,
until it was just
a dot in the sky.

Kirsty leaned against the branch
she'd landed on, trying to catch her
breath, and wondering what they
should do now. The petal was gone,
but they couldn't possibly fly after it
in such a gale.

After a few moments, the spell
wore off and the wind died down.

"Are you two all right?" Tia
asked Kirsty and Rachel. The girls
nodded and Tia sighed with relief.

"That wand is more powerful than I'd thought," she said. "Where has it sent my petal?"

The three of them scoured the sky, hoping to catch a glimpse of the orange petal, but they couldn't see any sign of it. Then Rachel noticed the goblins acting strangely on the ground.

They were running up and down,
staring at the sky. She glanced up to
see what they were looking at, and
saw the petal way above them, floating
down from a great height and drifting
back and forth on the breeze.

"Look! The goblins have spotted it!"
Rachel cried to the others. "Quick!"

The three fairies zoomed towards the falling petal, hoping to catch it before it fell into a goblin hand. But once again, the goblins saw them coming.

"Cast another spell!" they urged the one with the wand.

Kirsty braced herself as he pointed the wand up towards the fairies and shouted out another spell.

"Let's have an icy gale again. Blow, wind, blow, when I count to ten!"

Then he stood there, looking pleased with himself, until one of the other goblins nudged him. "Go on, then!" he yelled. "Count to ten, you idiot!"

"Oh, yes," the first goblin muttered. "One, two, three, four, five, six, seven-eight-nine-ten!" he counted at top speed. Then, "Go!" he shouted, with a loud cackle.

The Wrong End of the Stick

Rachel tensed all over, waiting for the freezing blast of wind to strike a second time. She could hardly bear to look, knowing she was about to be swept away by the gale all over again.

But then, to her great surprise, she heard Kirsty and Tia giggling. Rachel stared at her friends, and then followed

their gaze to see what they were
laughing at. They were looking
down at the goblins.

Once again, an icy wind was
streaming from the wand, but this time
it wasn't blowing towards the fairies.
The goblin hadn't realised that he was

holding the wand the wrong way round this time, so the wind that he'd meant for the fairies was actually blowing him and his friends away!

"Help!" they cried, as the gale swept them up and sent them tumbling along the ground. "What's happening?"

Kirsty gave a cheer, and then she and her friends swooped down to the magic petal which had just landed on the grass. Tia waved her wand, shrinking it to its Fairyland size, then whizzed up into the air with it, zooming a loop-the-loop in delight. "It's wonderful to have my petal back!" she beamed. "Thank you so much for helping me, girls!"

"Any time," Rachel smiled. "We're happy to help, Tia."

"I'd better take my petal back to Fairyland now," she said. "My sisters will be so pleased!" She flew above Kirsty and Rachel, showering them with orange fairy dust and turning them back into girls again.

"Thanks again," Tia sang. "See you soon!"

"Goodbye, Tia," Kirsty called, as the little fairy disappeared into thin air, with a shimmer of orange magic.

"That was fun," Rachel said happily as she and Kirsty headed back through the orchard.

"Yes it was," Kirsty agreed.

"Although I hope the goblins don't get any better at casting spells. I don't like them having a magic wand to use."

The girls came out of the orchard and headed along a footpath towards the house. As they walked past a large flowering bush, they heard cross voices. Curious, they peeped into the bush – and saw all of the goblins tangled in a heap!

Kirsty and Rachel looked at each other and burst out laughing. "It's going to take them a while to get out of there," Kirsty giggled.

They were crossing the lawn towards Blossom Hall when Rachel suddenly stopped walking and nudged Kirsty. "Kirsty, look," she said, pointing at one of the flowerbeds. "Those tulips look a bit, well, perkier than when we were here earlier."

Kirsty stared. Her friend was right. The tulips were all standing up proudly now, looking decidedly brighter and healthier than they had done before.

She grinned. "Tia's magic must be
working already!" she said in a low
voice. "And look at the gorgeous
orange ones. They definitely weren't
there before."

"They're beautiful," Rachel
said happily.

"There are still lots of bare patches of earth, though," Kirsty pointed out. "I really hope we can find the other magic petals soon."

Rachel nodded. "One thing's for sure," she said, linking arms with Kirsty, "we're in for a very exciting holiday week!"

The Petal Fairies

Tia the Tulip Fairy has got
her magic petal back. Now Rachel
and Kirsty must help

Pippa the Poppy Fairy

Win Rainbow Magic goodies!

In every book in the Rainbow Magic Petal Fairies series
(books 43-49) there is a hidden picture of a petal with a secret letter
in it. Find all seven letters and re-arrange them to make a special
Petal Fairies word, then send it to us. Each month we will put
the entries into a draw and select one winner to receive
a Rainbow Magic Sparkly T-shirt and Goody Bag!

Send your entry on a postcard to Rainbow Magic Fun Day
Competition, Orchard Books, 338 Euston Road, London NW1 3BH.
Australian readers should write to Hachette Children's Books,
Level 17/207 Kent Street, Sydney, NSW 2000.
New Zealand readers should write to Rainbow Magic Competition,
4 Whetu Place, Mairangi Bay, Auckland, NZ. Don't forget to
include your name and address. Only one entry per child.
Final draw: 30th April 2008.

Good luck!

Have you checked out the

website at:
www.rainbowmagic.co.uk

by Daisy Meadows

The Pet Keeper Fairies

The Fun Day Fairies

Coming soon:

All priced at £3.99. *Holly the Christmas Fairy, Summer the Holiday Fairy, Stella the Star Fairy, Kylie the Carnival Fairy, Paige the Pantomime Fairy* and *Flora the Fancy Dress Fairy* are priced at £5.99. *The Rainbow Magic Treasury* is priced at £12.99.
Rainbow Magic books are available from all good bookshops, or can be ordered direct from the publisher: Orchard Books, PO BOX 29, Douglas IM99 1BQ
Credit card orders please telephone 01624 836000
or fax 01624 837033 or visit our Internet site: www.wattspub.co.uk
or e-mail: bookshop@enterprise.net for details.

To order please quote title, author and ISBN and your full name and address.
Cheques and postal orders should be made payable to 'Bookpost plc.'
Postage and packing is FREE within the UK
(overseas customers should add £2.00 per book).
Prices and availability are subject to change.

Look out for the Dance Fairies!

Available Now!